# Joker

# Vanessa Star

JOKER

Published by MBI Publishing

www.mbipublishing.org

Copyright © 2019 by Vanessa Star

ISBN-13: 978-0-9976242-3-6

## Joker

Las Vegas! Could it be true? Lily's lips stretched into a happy smile. Life seemed like a fairy tale, full of adventures and little surprises! Why couldn't she be Cinderella? She'd had a simple life in her native Rouen, hadn't hoped for anything, worked hard and didn't lose hope, and finally met her Prince Charming! And he had brought her to his miracle world and made her his princess. Or maybe the Queen of Hearts? Lily giggled and put her toes under the Jacuzzi tub's strong jets. Yes, this comparison was more likely here, in Las Vegas!

The lilac aroma, emanating from the candles on the dressing-table, was mixing with the tender freshness of the bath foam. Soft classical music, probably Saint-Saens, was coming from the depth of the room, filling her mind with divine tranquility and blissful peace. Lily lazily reached for the glass of dry champagne on the Jacuzzi's side. Well, it was time to get ready. Today Phil was taking her to Celine Dion's concert—she had been dreaming of it for so long!

She carefully got out of the Jacuzzi and wrapped herself in a pale-yellow terry towel. What would she put on? It looked like Phil had bought a new outfit for her again. He was dressing her like a doll. And nothing but the best, the most expensive!

She impatiently tore the silk ribbon off the box and pulled out a long lilac evening dress and a violet velvet top. Pretty, she had to admit! But not her style at all. Lily looked for the tags, but there weren't any. Well, well. He must have cut them off not to embarrass her with the outrageous price. He was so caring and sweet! And also tall, handsome, and rich! Lily started to spin around the room in a slow waltz, pressing the lilac dress to her body. The cool silk was rustling in tune with the breezy music. Why had she decided that lilac was not her color?

*You need more class, little dummy! Only black for you, hah? Last century!* Have you *forgotten you're not a blond anymore? Your hair is auburn!* Lily stopped in front of the mirror and touched her new short auburn locks in disbelief. *So what! It's better this way!*

The salon, where Phil had taken her in New York, was so chic that she felt lost and could only produce a docile smile while the hairdresser in tight leather pants explained what he was going to do with her long blond hair. Then she simply closed her eyes and relaxed, hoping that Phil would like her even more with a new hairdo. It was his idea after all! After an hour and a half, the restless stylist, with a splendid smile, turned her to the mirror, and she saw the reflection of a stranger with short auburn hair. She gasped and almost asked, "Who is it?" Phil was already by her side expressing his admiration so clearly that she forced a smile. She almost got used to her

4

new image during the following weeks and even started to find a certain flare in it. Dammit, she was French and not some blonde cowgirl from the Midwest!

Well, the dress was lilac, so, she would need to add a touch of pale pink lipstick, and a little violet eyeshadow would do. Wait a moment! What about shoes and a purse? Lily flung open the closet—of course! The silver pumps would do marvelously. Hmmm, she needed a purse to match. A dilemma!

She knew that she didn't have a silver purse. Well, then she would buy it! She felt excited—this was a pretext to raid the luxurious shops of the hotel. What was it sitting on the lower shelf?

Her eyes stopped on the dress box. There was a pile of wrapping paper in it. *Let's check just in case. That's it!* Exactly the thing she needed! An elegant silver–colored clutch from Chanel, embroidered with beads, hidden in the bottom of the box. Lily fondled it like a toy. Phil had foreseen everything!

However, something was wrong. A slight, hardly sensible aroma of some strange perfume was coming from the purse. Could this purse have already been in someone's hands? There! One bead was missing in the corner. Where did Phil get it? Certainly not in a second-hand store. Too petty for him! Then maybe…Lily's heart squeezed. Could it be his ex-girlfriend's purse?

Lily sat down on the edge of the bed and opened it. Nothing special. A soft silk liner, a couple

6

of small pockets. Had it been simply returned to a store, and Phil bought it by chance? Couldn't he miss a detail or two occasionally? No, there was nothing to worry about.

*Okay, we can put the compact and the lipstick in this compartment. Perfect! And what is this?* A glossy tip was sticking from under the liner. What could it be? A photograph? Lily carefully pulled out a small picture, turned it over—and her heart plummeted. She was looking at a photo of a smiling Phil in a tuxedo and bow tie and…herself in this very silk lilac dress and the silver-colored purse in hand, with a huge Christmas tree in the background. On the bottom, she saw words printed in a red frame: "Happy New Year 2014! Rockefeller Center." This was impossible, simply un-re-al! She celebrated the New Year in Rouen, in the company of her two girlfriends, and besides, she had only met Phil last month! Delirium?!

She felt unwell. The picture slipped from her sweaty fingers. Lily slowly slid onto the carpet. What could it all mean?

*I have not been to Rockefeller Center! Never been! I know! It's not me! Not me!*

Well, if not her, then who?

Lily forced herself to get off the floor and carefully, as if it was a thorny cactus, picked up the picture with the tips of her fingers. She had a different smile on the photo, different lips, and she never folded her arms in such a prissy manner. Yes, certainly, it was another woman, but strikingly resembling her! With the same hairdo? And the dress? This very outfit? That was it! Of course! Phil selected it on purpose, just like her new hair color

8

and cut. And it meant… Lily covered her mouth with her hand, not to scream.

Could he be insane? Choosing women who look alike, dressing them in similar outfits, to resemble his…dead mother? Or sister? And then… Lily didn't even want to think what happened then. Tearing her old jeans and sweater from the closet, she hurried as if a murderer with an ax was already waiting by her door.

What did she really know about him? That he was a successful lawyer from Chicago dealing with some big corporate business? That he was well-off? Was it really so? Even if it was, it didn't mean he was not a psycho. Lily slipped on her moccasins, took a baseball cap from the upper shelf and hid her auburn hair under it.

What next? She stopped by the mirror, studied her reflection: eyes howling with terror, bright spots on her cheeks. This way she will soon go mad! Where was it that she was so hurrying to go? Escape? Where to? And then—there was no proof. The picture? Maybe it was his wife who had suddenly passed away from a terminal illness, and he simply wanted her, Lily, to resemble the deceased as much as possible? So what was so scary about it?

Lily drank a little cold coffee left over from lunch and decisively started the search. She did not know what she was looking for, just followed her inner instinct. She quickly went through Phil's suitcase and travel bag, did not find anything unusual, and neatly put everything back. What was left? Lily glanced around the spacious one-bedroom

10

suite. She should probably go through his pockets, but a chill in her back was pushing her to the door. Time was running out! Phil could return any moment.

On the desk, under the hotel flyers, she found Phil's appointment book. Lily sat on the soft bench and started looking through it. Again, nothing special. Business meeting notes, names, telephone numbers. On the second page, there were several phone numbers without names. Lily quickly copied them in her notebook just in case.

There, their trip schedule: New York, Washington D.C., Las Vegas. Everything was correct. The arrival time matched. There was a note about yesterday's dinner and today's concert. Hmmm, where was their trip to the Grand Canyon? It was planned for Thursday, right? And the Cirque du Soleil show on Friday? Instead, under "Friday" it was written in small letters: "Barbados via Miami, 18:50." Lily feverishly turned the page. No Los Angeles, where they were supposedly going. Instead, some Spanish names: Las Perlas, Avenida de la Concepcion...

Lily quickly grabbed her old leather wallet with money and documents, threw big dark glasses on her nose, and closed the suite's door behind her. Her brain was working fast.

*Has he decided to pass me like her, that gal with a haircut, for some shady purpose? And then skip town with her? Like hell! We shall see who will be a six, and who—a queen!* True, at present they have outplayed her. Her fake King turned out to be just a Joker and was mockingly showing her his tongue. Cinderella! Prince Charming! A fairytale!

How about jail? For sure, those two were working on some sting, and she had been chosen as the bait. What a fool!

An express elevator whisked Lily to the first floor. The casino sounds and smells surrounded her. Where should she look for him? He said he would be playing poker. Fat chance! He must be having a date with that woman now. They could be anywhere in this huge, roaring, sparkling, giggling city of entertainment.

She scoured every corner of the casino. Phil was not there. One floor up was the most interesting in the Venetian hotel: the streets and squares of Venice, the Grand Canal with real gondolas, the street actors and live statues, and this entire glamor under a painted sky with clouds, almost real.

She ran the perimeter of the Grand Canal, dropped by the boutiques and small shops selling bric-a-brac from all over the world, and finally landed on a bench, exhausted. Phil was nowhere. She did not feel like storming to other hotels, and she definitely wouldn't return to her room. She could go to the airport, buy a ticket on the next flight to New York, and return to Paris the following day. So that was it? Were all her dreams just a cruel joke?

She leaned her head on the back of the bench and closed her eyes. Just recently, she and Phil had been flying to Las Vegas, and making such plans! How attentive he was, courteous… pouring champagne for her, covering her feet with a blanket.

Phil's velvet baritone sounded in Lily's head.

"Baby, you'll love Las Vegas, I know. The hotel we're staying in, The Venetian, will dazzle you. Can you imagine Venice under a roof?"

She giggled quietly and stroked the tips of his fingers.

"Imagine the ice cream they have there! Better than in Venice itself, trust me! And the restaurants and cafes! I have a couple of favorite places, and we'll go there for sure…"

Stop! Lily sharply opened her eyes. That was right! She remembered those names: Canaletto and Tintoretto. They dined in Canaletto the day before; it meant Tintoretto was left. She dashed to look for the hotel map. Here it was, Tintoretto, very near, at the turn of the canal.

She spotted them right away through a huge window. A table by the wall. Phil was sitting with his back to the door, leaning a bit forward, and talked, at times looking around. Lily couldn't make out his companion very well, just saw a gray hat, tinted glasses and a sleeve of a blue dress. A short chestnut lock showed from under her hat, the lady tucked it in, smiled, and folded her arms in a prissy gesture, like in that damned photo! She must be disguising herself, but there was no doubt—it was, in fact, her, Lily's unknown double!

The next second Lily was already entering the café, grabbing an Italian paper from the stand by the entrance. She walked up to the bar and with an exaggerated Italian accent, ordered a large cup of cappuccino and a piece of Tiramisu cake. The waiter broke into a wide smile and shot out probably the only thing he knew in Italian: "Prego, signora!"

Lily pulled her hat lower over her eyes, took her tray, and slowly made her way to the table behind Phil.

"Are you sure everything is covered? There will be no misfires?" The lady's anxious whisper came to Lily quite clearly, and she mentally thanked God.

Phil was speaking a lot softer, and Lily could hardly make out his words. She concealed herself with the newspaper, forced a gulp of coffee, and picked deliciously looking Tiramisu with a fork. It was dangerous to move closer.

"I've already explained everything to you!" Phil's voice grew louder. He threw his napkin on the table. He was definitely irritated.

"But where is the guarantee? Only the violet dress and auburn hair? What if somebody doubts?"

The woman in the blue dress continued her nervous inquiry.

A chill went down Lily's spine. It was clear they were talking about her.

"Listen to me again," Phil's voice was coming and going as if somebody was fumbling with the volume. "Remember, nobody has your DNA sample, or even your medical records, right? You did a perfect job covering your tracks! With the rest, they will have to trust me. Only I can identify the body here." He finished on a high note, quite satisfied with himself.

His companion was still talking, but Lily did not hear any more. Her teeth were clattering so loudly, that she did not dare drink any more coffee, quietly pushed the chair back, and made herself slowly and casually leave the café. Her only impulse was to run—as fast and as far as possible. She turned the corner, went to the nearest restroom, locked herself in a cabin, and leaned back on the door. She found a pack of Gitanes in the depth of her old handbag and took out a cigarette.

What she heard could mean only one thing: they wanted to kill her, and Phil had to identify the body as the body of that woman from the picture. Why? For what purpose? Her natural curiosity overtook primordial fear. She simply had to dig to the bottom of this story! She was not the fool they took her for! What if… Lily tore the cigarette and threw it into the toilet, flushed it, came up to the sink, washed her face, and once again looked at herself in the mirror. It would be hard to recognize her, especially in dark glasses. In this cap, she resembled a boy from a working suburb of Paris.

What if she played her own game? *We'll see who will be that last Joker, who laughs.*

She had to hurry.

Luckily, the couple was still sitting in the café. Lily stared at the shop windows, feigning interest. In a few minutes, Phil exited, waved to his companion, and quickly headed to the bridge over the canal. Lily dashed a glance behind—the lady continued to sit at the table, deep in thought. Perfect. In three strides, Lily crossed the ornate bridge, and found herself at the corner of St. Mark's square, a little behind Phil, who was examining the collection of Venetian masks, throwing around quick glimpses. As if, he was looking for somebody. An accomplice? Lily leaned back against the painted house and followed the direction of Phil's glance.

Two bucks in Hawaiian shirts stood by the stage with a live statue. They were clearly interested in Phil. In a few minutes, Phil took his cell phone from his pocket, and the pair in colorful shirts came closer to Lily. She lazily walked up to the kiosk selling things made of colored glass. From there, she hoped to hear at least scraps of Phil's conversation. However, she was a lot luckier. Apparently, his counterpart did not hear very well, and Phil was practically yelling.

"Yes, yes, Limo to the main entrance, yes, today, at 6 pm, repeat! Yes, a white limousine".

People started to look at him, but he, as if nothing happened, put away his phone, cast a glance at the Hawaiian shirts and, whistling, walked away from the square.

"It's turning out well!" Phil thought to himself. "These idiots always dress up like scarecrows. Funny! Oh, well. They probably consider me a total boob as well. All the better. The main thing, they caught the bait and likely, they'll use it. I hope Julie will not interfere! It's good she doesn't know the details. She's too impulsive! No, let her be a bit nervous. God willing, tomorrow everything will be behind us." He decisively headed to the elevators. "It's time to take care of our little Lily."

Lily quickly returned to Tintoretto cafe. The lady in the gray hat was finishing her coffee. Lily had to hurry. Well, she would have to try all the phone numbers on her list. Good girl, she wrote down all of them just in case! Lily dialed the first number, watching her "double" through the window. There was no ring. Hang up. The second number, the third—there! A melodic music came, and the lady took a miniature phone from an elegant blue handbag.

"Hello!" Her voice did not resemble Lily's at all.

Lily walked further away. Extra precaution wouldn't hurt.

"Hello, my name is Lily. You know me, but not personally. Don't hang up, otherwise, you'll greatly regret it!" She talked very fast, covering her mouth with her hand. "Yes, yes, you heard me right, it's me that very Lily, the fool, the French woman who you wanted to set up with your pal Phil. Sorry, it won't work out! I know everything!"

The lady gasped and asked quietly,

"Everything?"

"Everything, your entire plan!" A lot depended on this bluff, and Lily tried her best to bring a shade of metal to her voice. "Listen to me carefully. Don't even dream of contacting Phil. I'm watching him, and if he answers his cell, I'll disappear immediately, and forever!"

No answer followed.

"I have a proposal for you, miss. A good one. But only for you alone! Do you understand me?"

"Y-yes."

"Perfect. You'll meet me tonight, and we'll discuss everything. If not, I'll disappear."

"B-but how shall we both…" Doubt sounded in her voice.

"Don't worry; you can continue your disguise. It won't hinder us. So, tonight at 6 pm in the hall, near the main entrance to the hotel. Do you understand me?"

"Yeah."

"I think we'll recognize each other easily," Lily chuckled. "And don't you try to get ahold of Phil. I'll deal with him. Otherwise, you'll never find me, believe me!"

That was it. Now she could only hope she made a convincing impression on this miss. Lily darted to the elevators, grabbing a Las Vegas souvenir in the first shop she passed.

"No change, thanks!"

She carefully opened the suite door and held her breath. Silence. Very good.

Phil appeared from behind the bedroom door, holding that very lilac dress in his hands.

"Honey, I was so worried! Where have you been? And… what are you wearing? It's vulgar!"

Thank God, she already took off her cap and fixed her hair on the way.

'Phil, can't I even go shopping?" She squeezed a tense smile, made herself approach him and kiss his cheek.

"So where have you been?" Worry slipped in his voice.

"You know, I got stuck in the shops right near the entrance to the second floor. They have so much there! Here, I bought a plate. Isn't it cute? I'll go change. We have to leave soon, don't we?"

"Sure, and hurry, darling, we don't have much time."

"What time is the concert?" She asked as innocently as she could, heading for the bathroom. "Oh, by the way, how are we going there? By taxi? Is it far?"

"It's near, but I have a surprise for you," Phil smiled smugly. "We'll go in a limo."

"Re-e-ally?" She tried to portray delighted amazement, sticking her head from behind the half-opened door. "In a real black limo?"

27

He sat sprawling in a chair, lazily sipping whiskey from a low glass, a smug expression on his face. How on earth could she ever have liked him?!

"In a real white limo, my girl! Ours will be white!"

When they were leaving the room, Lily looked smashing in her lilac outfit. She carried quite a sizeable plastic bag in her hands.

Phil winced with displeasure.

"Why do you need this bag? It spoils the whole impression."

"Don't argue, my dear! I know perfectly well how cold it can be at those shows. They set the air conditioners here on high. So, I may need my top and the shawl."

He only shrugged his shoulders.

As soon as they stepped out of the elevator on the first floor, Lily made a guilty grimace and whispered in Phil's ear,

"I have to go to the bathroom. I'll be right back!"

"We have very little time! Can't you wait till the concert?"

"No, sorry, I can't. I'll be quick!"

The time was truly short. She had noticed the restroom earlier. It had two exits, about twenty feet apart. Phil sat down at a slot machine near the first exit.

Lily quickly plunged into a cabin, pulled off her dress, slipped on jeans and a sweater, and covered her hair with a cap. Perfect. A blond girl by the sink was laughing, trying to engage the tap, cursing in Italian.

"This way! Ecco!" Lily pressed a button. "Do you speak English? It took me some time to figure it out."

In a moment, they exited together through the second door, eagerly chatting in Italian. Lily once again complimented herself on her language skills.

As soon as they turned the corner, Lily threw a quick goodbye to the Italian girl and dashed to the main entrance. Here is our lady. Still in her hat and dark glasses, only the blue dress gave way to a gray pantsuit. Now speed was all that mattered. She had to beat the clock.

"Don't be surprised by the way I'm dressed," Lily started right off the bat. "We don't need anybody to recognize you or me now."

The lady looked her over from top to bottom with astonishment.

"Where is Phil?"

"Don't worry; he won't bother us today." Lily tried to make her smile as ominous as possible. "You'll go out to the curb now and get into a white limo. It's waiting right by the door. It will take you to Caesar's Palace. I'll follow you in another car. We'll meet in the lobby right by the main entrance and discuss a new plan. This will be just our party!"

"Very well!" *This girl turned out to be a lot smarter than Phil thought.* One could not trust a man, even such an industrious man as Phil. She would have to solve everything on her own. Maybe it was for the better! Julie made for the door, squeezing the gun in her purse. In a moment, a chauffeur in a livery was opening the white limousine's door for her.

Phil was already worried out of his wits. What was this girl doing so long in the restroom? God forbid, she could be having a fit of diarrhea. He chuckled and came up to the ladies' room door.

"Madam," he politely addressed an elderly woman with strings of large beads on her massive neck. "My fiancée went into this restroom quite a long time ago. I'm very worried. Would you be so kind to see if she is all right? She is a tall, pretty girl with short auburn hair in a long lilac dress."

"But certainly, young man, I'll help you," the woman gently smiled at him.

When she came out and declared that no such young lady was present in the bathroom, Phil panicked and rushed to look for a hotel employee. She too, after thoroughly searching all the cabins, reassured Phil there was nobody resembling his fiancée there.

Phil stormed toward the main entrance, pushing his way. A crowd was thronging in the lobby, but Lily was not there. He charged out into the street. Taxis, limos, minibusses, private cars were driving up to the main entrance. There was no white limo there. His last hope was a porter.

Phil sprang toward him, pulling out a ten dollar banknote on the way.

"Yes, there was a white limo, and some lady, I reckon, got into it, and it left. About ten minutes ago. I wouldn't testify to it. You see yourself, sir, what's going on here. I beg your pardon," the porter touched his cap's visor with a white-gloved finger and switched his attention to the next taxi.

Well! She must have gotten into the limo after all! Could it have worked? Why did she pass him by? Didn't notice him? Misunderstood something? Did it matter after all? It was even easier this way— he didn't have to invent an urgent phone call to avoid getting into the limo with her. Now, all that was left was to wait.

The next day, in the afternoon, Phil exited the morgue with a mournful expression on his face. The bright Las Vegas sun blinded him, as soon as he opened the door to the street. He took his dark glasses from his coat pocket and brushed an unseen dust particle off his jacket sleeve. Trying to keep a sorrowful expression, he slowly descended the steps and walked to the café on the opposite side of the square. Just in case some shrewd journalist may be hiding somewhere nearby, Phil had to observe the proprieties.

His soul was singing. It worked! It couldn't be better! He identified the body and signed the papers. In fact, he didn't look that closely, when the employee folded back the sheet from the gurney. Even one glance was enough—it was her, Lily! He even squeezed out a tear, and his hands were trembling when he signed his testimony. Everything was proper. How else could it be? He identified her as his girlfriend, Julie Archers. So from now on, he was officially stricken by grief, almost a widower.

Well, truly, the whole scheme went like clockwork. Lady Luck must have been on his side. Phil sipped tequila from a small shot glass. Where was Julie, by the way? He couldn't get a hold of Julie since last night. She checked out of the hotel, as planned. Her telephone was disconnected. Maybe, as a precaution? Nothing to worry about! They would meet at the airport in the evening. In Barbados, they would not need to hide anymore. And for now—he could bet three or four hundred on roulette. A carnivorous smile curved his lips. Today was his lucky day!

He went out into the street and headed to the taxi stand.

"Not so fast, my dear!" A tiny hand tapped the back of his shoulder, and Phil broke into a cold sweat. He could easily recognize this accent among the crowd.

"Don't turn around just yet, let's go around the corner."

The girl tore the dark glasses off her face. Phil, hardly breathing, glanced over her entire shapely figure: charcoal jeans, black tee-shirt, moccasins. Julie couldn't stand black; she said it was a funeral color.

"Still not recognizing me, messier?" She pulled a hairpin out of her jeans pocket, lifted the hair on the back of her head. "It'll take a long time to grow my hair back, but it's okay, I'll wait, it's worth it, right, my Prince? Yes, yes, it's me, Lily, your "find," your "bait," or whatever else you called me with that doll of yours?" She was almost screaming.

He quickly looked around.

"Don't be afraid, darling, nobody's interested in the two of us anymore, right? She—your Julie—is lying there, in the morgue, with two bullets, one in her spine, another in the back of her head. A signature style of the Chicago mafia, that's what's written in the papers, right?" From her backpack,

Lily took a crumbled paper with a half-page headline: "Mafia Collects Debts! Julie Archers, who stole millions from the Mob, is killed!"

"Wanted to trick the mafia? It didn't work! Tell me, Phil, were you looking for a girl resembling Julie on purpose, or it happened by chance? Keeping silent? Well, we'll have a ton of time to discuss everything. I think it was by chance. I remember how your eyes glowed when you saw me the first time in the bank in Rouen. It was then that the devilish plan came to your mind—to substitute me as Julie to the mafia, right?

"I," Phil finally squeezed out. "I don't understand what you are talking about."

Lily took his hand with a smile.

"Phil, don't waste your time! The newspapers give an exhaustive report about your girlfriend: how she was a secret "accountant" for the Chicago mafia, how her protector was killed—Big Bill, right? And how a large amount of their money disappeared from the accounts together with her. They would find her anyway, and she knew it. So don't grieve, pal! We have a lot to discuss. You must be dying to find out how she got into that white limo instead of me?"

She led him slowly down the alley.

"And I'd like to listen to your story, sweetie! How did you manage to stay in the shadows all this time? Will you tell me? We have a ton of time now. By the way, when is our flight to Barbados?"

Phil stopped abruptly.

"Why are you so surprised? Everything will go as planned. Tomorrow we'll be in the bank on Avenida de la Concepcion. All the accounts are in Julie's name, right? She would never have trusted you with such money! But then again, names and

banks can differ, but my appearance cannot be

replaced. You must have a nice new photo ID for

me, right? Let's hurry, cowboy, we still have to buy

some beach attire!" The End

www.ingramcontent.com/pod-product-compliance
Lightning Source LLC
Chambersburg PA
CBHW020607130626
46552CB00007B/3092